Soonchild

SOONCHILD

Russell Hoban

illustrated by Alexis Deacon

CANDLEWICK PRESS

Text copyright © 2012 by Russell Hoban
Illustrations copyright © 2012 by Alexis Deacon

First U.S. edition 2012

Library of Congress Cataloging-in-Publication Data is available.

Library of Congress Catalog Card Number pending

ISBN 978-0-7636-5920-2

12 13 14 15 16 17 SCP 10 9 8 7 6 5 4 3 2 1

Printed in Humen, Dongguan, China

This book was typeset in New Century Schoolbook.
The illustrations were done in charcoal and pencil.

Candlewick Press
99 Dover Street
Somerville, Massachusetts 02144

visit us at www.candlewick.com

For my grandchildren:
Benjamin; Daniel; Jacob;
Elias; Ilana; Alisa; Paul;
Adam; Emma; Holly; Samuel;
Megan; Anna; Stella

R. H.

AUTHOR'S NOTE

The North in my mind is partly the one from my childhood, when I used to send away for Canadian Railway
maps and delight in the blue expanse of Hudson Bay.
This North has since joined up with the one in the BBC's
Kingdom of the Ice Bear, where I met the barnacle-geese
children. My dog-handling comes from Google. The skidoos were gliding around in my unreliable memory and
the word was confirmed by Bruce Bergen of Thomas
Motors Ltd. in Nipawin, Saskatchewan. The stiff nose
hairs and brittle eyeballs date from my childhood sled-
ding in Pennsylvania.

"When you boil up a
Big-Dream Brew, you
better be ready to drink to
the bottom of the cup."

NANUQ

SIXTEEN·FACE JOHN: HIS·NORTH

Maybe you think there isn't any north where you are. Maybe it's warm and cozy and outside the window the street is full of cars or maybe there's just emptiness and a train whistle. There aren't any Inuit or dogsleds, nothing like that. But in your mind there is a North.

There's a north where it's so cold that your nose hairs get stiff and your eyeballs get brittle and your face hurts and your hands will freeze if you leave them uncovered too long. A north where the white wind blows, where the night wind wails with the voices of the cold and lonesome dead. Where the ice bear walks alone and he's never lost. Where the white wolf comes trotting, trotting on the paths of the living, the paths of the dead. Where the snowy owl

1

drifts through the long twilight without a sound. Where the raven speaks his word of black.

In this north there's a place on the shore of the great northern bay with forty or fifty huts and a co-op and some boats and some of those motorized sleds they call skidoos. Some of the people still live by hunting and fishing but many have jobs and buy their food at the co-op.

In the winter it's just a huddle of dark shapes in an endless whiteness under a gray sky. The gray air shimmering where stovepipes stick out of roofs. The smell of far away and the barking of dogs. If you don't live there it's just some place that's noplace.

Some of the spirits of the place have moved away, others have died. Yes, spirits die. They die when they're no longer taken notice of, no longer spoken to. But there are still some who live on the best they can and answer if they're spoken to in the proper way.

This place with the forty or fifty huts and the co-op and so on was Sixteen-Face John's place. Sixteen-Face John was the big fear man. Nobody was as afraid as he was, nobody had so many faces to be afraid with. If a thing was too much for him to face with his first face, he would go to his second one and so on down the line. What I'm saying is that he had sixteen different faces for looking at what scared him. I can't tell you how he did it because he himself didn't know how he did it, it was just what he did.

FACES ONE TO FOUR

John's first face was the ordinary face you'd see him walking around with. That was his Hi face, the one he said hello with. Face Two was What? Face Three was Really? Face Four was Well, Well.

FACES FIVE TO EIGHT

Face Five was Go On! Face Six was You Don't Mean It. Face Seven was You Mean It? Face Eight was That'll Be The Day.

FACES NINE TO TWELVE

Face Nine was What Day Will That Be? Face Ten was It Can't Be That Bad. Face Eleven was Can It Be That Bad? Face Twelve was I Don't Believe It.

FACES THIRTEEN TO SIXTEEN

Face Thirteen was I Believe It. Face Fourteen was This Is Serious. Face Fifteen was What I'm Seeing Is What It Is. Face Sixteen was What It's Seeing Is What I Am.

THE SCAREDNESS OF JOHN

John never told anyone the names of his faces, that was his secret. Except for two special times in his life he'd never gone all the way to Face Sixteen because he was afraid to leave himself with no face to go to in case of really big trouble. Most things he could handle with faces One to Seven although once in a while he'd have to go as far as Nine or Ten, like the time he almost got trampled by a herd of musk-oxen (Face Nine) or the time when his wife, No Problem, went for him with an ax (Face Ten).

John was scared pretty much all the time. Sometimes he was so scared that he thought he might have to get a helper to take on some of the scaredness but then he'd say to himself, "Come on, John, you can do it, you've always got another face to work with, so stay with it, you are the big fear man."

People used to ask him how he got to be so scared. He told them that he started out scared and as time went on he got a little more scared every day. "There's so much to be afraid of. Listen to the wind, how it's moaning with the voices of the dead, the cold and lonesome dead. They're afraid the same as I am."

What of? they wanted to know.

4

"They're afraid the world will go away and so am I," said John. "Aren't you?"

No, they said, they weren't.

"Don't you, like, feel it slipping away?" said John. "Like your pants falling down?"

Maybe, they said, John felt that way because his pants were falling down. He had a big belly and a small bottom so that was bound to happen, what did he expect.

"Forget about my pants," said John. "You ever think about what you're seeing?"

How? they said. What did he mean?

"When you're looking at something there's a picture in your eyes of what you're looking at, yes? Like the picture in my eyes right now is the co-op with snow on the roof except for a little black circle around the stovepipe. The heat from the stovepipe is shimmering on the air. There are dogsleds and skidoos parked by the co-op and people going in and out. This is the world in my eyes.

"This world is there and it's there as long as my eyes are open. Maybe it's flickering a little like a movie, I'm not sure. I close my eyes and it's gone, no more world. When I open my eyes it's there again. You'll tell me that world is always there. OK, it's there so far. But what if too many people close their eyes at the same time, or go to sleep and don't dream this world, what then?" That worried John, he didn't like to think about it.

So anyhow, this Sixteen-Face John was a shaman, what

they call an *angakoq*. People would come to him to find out where the good hunting was or wanting him to take away a sickness or make somebody fall in love with them and he would do whatever they needed him to do. He would dream or go into a trance or travel to wherever he had to go and come back with some kind of answer. Or he would go to the animal in him, whichever one was right for the job. Sometimes he got a good result, sometimes not. You win some, you lose some. But John was the local shaman and he did all the shaman work around where he lived.

John came from a long line of shamans. His mother was Stay With It and his father was Go Anywhere. His mother's mother was Never Give Up and her father was Try Anything. His father's mother was Do It Now and his father's father was Whatever Works. His mother's grandmother was Where Is It? and his father's grandmother was Don't Miss Anything. His mother's grandfather was Everything Matters and his father's grandfather was Go All The Way. They were all shamans and they were all dead but they were still busy with the living because the living are the link between the dead and the unborn and the dead have to work all the time to pass along to the unborn all the things they're going to need. Like Look For It. Like Make It Happen. That kind of thing. Maybe you think you're doing it all by yourself but it's the dead working in you. They simply have no rest, the dead. Life is hard and death is hard, nothing is easy.

6

Sixteen-Face John's parents and grandparents had taught him how to find good hunting and how to heal the sick and the other things shamans needed to know. They taught him dreams and trances, magic songs and dances. They taught him how to look behind the little round mirror in the eye of the raven, how to hear the blue-green song of the ice bear, and how to travel on the inside of the night, even in the daytime—things that you can't learn from books, they have to pass from one generation to the next by word of mouth.

The most important thing they taught him was how to talk to spirits. In the ice bear, in the seal, in each kind of animal lives the spirit for all the animals of that kind. When a hunter kills an animal the spirit must be spoken to in the right way, it has to be shown respect if the hunter wants his luck to hold. Spirits like a lot of attention. They like to be admired, and the shaman has to know how to please them so they'll be friendly to his people.

These animal spirits don't just live in the ice bear and the seal and so on, they live in people too. And not just animal spirits but the spirits of everything else— rocks and oceans and the night and everything there is. Everything lives in everybody, deep down and way, way back where there are no words. Breath and sounds but no words. Where the strangeness is. If you can get your brain out of the way your mind will take you there and the spirits will talk to you in words. Not everybody can get there. Those who can are shamans.

John was a good shaman because there was nothing he was afraid to be afraid of. You name it and he's looked at it with however many faces it took to see what it was and how to deal with it. Famine, sickness, death, jealousy, love, hate, boils and veruccas, whatever. He did it year after year but after a certain number of years he began to have bad dreams.

Sixteen-Face John dreamed of colors that had no names and all kinds of shapes and sounds shooting past him at great speed. He heard the voices of stones and seabirds and ravens, he heard the voices of the dead of many places and many times. He dreamed of great hollow spaces where all the colors were white and the white was full of blackness that had no time in it. He dreamed of a dry red place where everything was dancing and nothing was alive. In all these dreams he couldn't see his hands and he couldn't hear himself speak, he couldn't take hold of anything and he had no voice.

The dreams were bad enough but the whispering was worse. The whispering was in his head and he heard it when he was sleeping and when he was awake. It was the kind of sound a glacier might make as it slides toward the sea, inching in the night. He couldn't make out any words and he was thankful for that.

John tried looking at the whispering with two or three

faces and he couldn't make out the shape of it but there was something about it that took the heart out of him. It was so personal. It scared him all the way to Face Nine, What Day Will That Be? Then he stopped looking because he wasn't ready to go all the way with it.

There was no doubt in John's mind that whatever was doing the whispering was waiting for him in one of those places where shamans have to go so he thought it would be a good idea to stay out of those places. Naturally when he stopped going to those places he stopped getting the results he used to get and people stopped coming to him. Sixteen-Face John still called himself a shaman but he took to drinking Coca-Cola and watching TV with his feet up and reading magazines with centerfolds in them. The whispering was still there but he made sure there was always a lot of other noise on top of it.

John did a little hunting and fishing and trapping when he had to, with a skidoo instead of a dogsled. He also carved figures out of whalebone and ivory and antler and bone and stone which he sold through the co-op. His wife, No Problem, prepared the skins from his hunting and she made and sold those skin boots they call *kamiks* and those light inner parkas they call *atigis*. Between them John and No Problem made a living.

What John looked like: he wasn't as young as he used to be and he wasn't as old as he was hoping to be. He was shorter than he was tall. His Number One Face had the kind of smile you right away distrusted. You've already heard about his big belly and his little bottom and his falling-down pants. His most outstanding feature was his smell. It was strong and it was special. Later you'll hear how John met Nanuq and it could well be that John only came out of it alive because of his smell—it made Nanuq stop and ask himself, What kind of man is this?

John was a good carver. The figures he carved were all strange ones, spirits and shamans and weird animals. One thing he never carved was an owl. Mostly he just felt around for what the whalebone or ivory or stone wanted. Around the time this story tells of, he picked up some whalebone, maybe it was from a rib. It was all gray and weathered with the fibers showing and he could feel some kind of shape inside it talking to him.

John said to the whalebone that he would do what it wanted. He didn't do his carving in the house that time, he took the whalebone and his knife and a hand adze and went out on the gray rocks of the shore. With the adze he started feeling for the shape while the whispering in his head got louder and the blade began to move by itself. When the adze had roughed in the shape John didn't like it very much but he took his knife and went on with it and the knife started moving by itself too. When John felt like stopping for a while he tried to put the knife down but he couldn't let go of it so he closed his eyes and didn't look at what the knife was doing until the carving was finished.

10

When the figure was done he wished he hadn't done it but he told himself that really the adze and the knife had done it by themselves. John had never heard of anybody else making a figure that way and it seemed to him to be an unlucky thing to do. John thought it would be better if nobody saw that figure so he hid it between two big rocks on the shore above the tide line.

WHAT DEEPGUY TOLD JOHN

That place on the shore was a regular spirit hangout. They liked the curves and hollows of those big rocks, they liked the dance of the stillness in the stone, they liked the song of its silence.

After he hid the ugly figure John was walking along the shore with the whispering getting louder in his head. There was a flickering in the air and he knew it was a spirit. He couldn't quite see it but he heard it in his head.

"Hi," said the spirit. "I'm Deepguy. I was having a snooze in the whalebone when you started with the adze so I helped you finish the job."

"It's a big honor for me to meet you, Mr. Deepguy," said John. "Thank you for letting us take beluga and narwhal."

"You're welcome," said the Deepguy. "You have good manners although you smell a little stronger than necessary."

"I had a shower no more than two months ago," said John. "I can't wash too often because it breaks my concentration. I have a lot on my mind."

"I'm about to give you more," said Deepguy.

"Before you do that," said John, "can I ask you very respectfully why you made that figure of me-notme so ugly?"

"*You* did that," said Deepguy. "You gave the figure a bad shape because *you're* in bad shape."

"Well, you know," said John, "a shaman is not like other people."

"Don't give me that," said Deepguy. "I've been looking into your shaman work and for a long time it hasn't amounted to diddly-poo. What I'm saying to you now is, pull up your pants and suck in your gut and get ready for something big."

"I don't think I can handle anything big," said John. "I'm not the shaman I used to be."

"Used-to-be won't cut it," said Deepguy. "This is a whole new ballgame."

"Why me?" said John. Tears were running down his face and he had to blow his nose.

"It has to be you because you're the only one there is."

"But the world is full of other people," whimpered John.

"And every one of them is the only one there is. How does that grab you?"

"Hard," said John. "Only I don't know what you mean."

"The world is a very slippery thing," said Deepguy. "And if all you only ones don't hold tight it could slip out of your hands like an eel. Got it?"

"So what should I do?"

"Go home and it will come to you," said Deepguy, and he wasn't there anymore.

John didn't feel much like going home, he was afraid of what might come to him there, but finally he went. Slowly.

Before John went home he took a rock and tried to smash the ugly figure but the rock bounced up and gave him a bloody nose.

WHAT SOONCHILD TOLD NO PROBLEM

No Problem was a big, strong woman with the kind of face that made you not want to make her angry. She used to beat all the boys at wrestling when she was a girl but now that she was a grown woman she spent most of her time scraping hides and making *kamiks* and *atigis* and that kind of thing.

So here she was with her big belly. When people asked her if she wanted a boy or a girl she said she wanted a girl. "I could use some help around here," she said.

Winter and spring had passed and now it was already summer. No Problem called the child inside her Soonchild because it would soon be time for the child to come out. She was sure it was a girl because she could feel she was like her mother, you wouldn't want to make her angry. She was stubborn too, she wouldn't kick or do the usual unborn things.

No Problem's mother, Take It Easy, said, "Take it easy, No. Soonchilds all have their little ways of keeping you guessing."

No Problem's friend, Way To Go, said, "Soonchild's going to do it her way, so you've got to flow with the go, even if it's a slow go."

"When, when, when, hey?" said No Problem to her belly. "When a little kick, when? Eight moons have filled and emptied, the ninth moon is already half full, and this child, my first child after all these years, is doing nothing at all. Surely it's time for a little kick, yes? A little 'Hello, here I am.' How about it?"

But Soonchild still didn't kick.

"This child is like a stone in my belly," said No Problem. "She isn't doing what she ought to be doing, she isn't getting ready to come out into the world. I know she's alive because I can feel her thinking and her thoughts are getting heavier and heavier. What's she thinking about? Such a young child shouldn't be doing all that heavy thinking, it worries me."

"Take it easy," said Take It Easy.

"Please stop saying that," said No Problem to her mother. "If I take it any easier I'll jump out of my skin."

"That's no way to go," said Way To Go.

"Look out or I'll give you a way to go with my foot in your backside," said No Problem.

No Problem decided to talk to her husband about her problem when he came home. She had seen him go out with the adze and the knife he used for carving and she was used to his ways so she didn't mind how long it took him and she went on cleaning fish while Take It Easy and Way To Go were scraping hides and singing a song they'd made up:

> *Sorry, Mr. White Fox, sorry, old friend,*
> *Everything's better with Coca-Cola,*
> *We want a Walkman and a video.*
> *Sorry that we took your skin,*
> *Got to bring some money in,*
> *Got to get a Walkman and a video.*
> *Sorry, Mr. Polar Bear,*
> *Sorry that we took your hair,*
> *Everything's better with Coca-Cola.*

While they worked they could hear a song coming from the loudspeaker in the co-op:

Lotsa hotsa pizza, baby,
want it to go,
Lotsa hotsa pizza, baby,
roll out the dough,
Lotsa hotsa pizza, baby,
want it to go.

"I could go for a pizza," said Way To Go.

"Way To Go," said No Problem. So they all knocked off for a pizza break. No Problem had hers with seal topping, Take It Easy had hers with char and Way To Go had a plain one, blubber and kelp.

WHAT SOONCHILD TOLD JOHN

While No Problem and the others were having pizza at the co-op John snuck home, got a Coke from the icebox, turned on the TV, put his feet up, and watched baseball while he drank his Coke. He was trying to convince himself that nothing big was going to happen.

There was no getting away from it though. No Problem's belly showed up and she was right behind it. "Listen," she said to John. "You're not only my husband, you're my local shaman." The way she said it made John hitch up his pants, suck in his gut, and go to Face Four, Well, Well.

"You're supposed to know all kinds of shaman things," said No Problem.

John backed up to Face Three, Really? He was hoping to get out from under anything too heavy. "Sometimes I do and sometimes I don't," he said.

"Well, this better be sometimes you do," said No Problem. "I have a problem, a big one."

"What is it?" said John.

"It's right there in front of you, also in front of me."

"This is something big all right," said John. He could feel himself sliding toward Face Ten, It Can't Be That Bad, but he dug in his heels and tried not to look too far ahead. "What month are you in?"

"Around here we say moons," said No Problem. It was bottom of the ninth with bases loaded but she turned off the TV.

"OK, what moon?" said John.

"Bottom of the ninth but this child is not getting ready to come out into the world," said No Problem. "She doesn't move, she doesn't kick, she's like a stone in my belly but I know she's alive because I can feel her thinking and her thoughts get heavier all the time."

"How do you know it's a she?"

"I just know, that's all."

"What's she thinking about?"

"Don't ask me, ask *her*. She won't talk to me."

John knelt down beside No Problem's belly. "Hello!" he said. "Soonchild, can you hear me?"

"No need to shout," said Soonchild. Her voice didn't seem to be coming from No Problem's belly, it sounded as if it was coming from giant speakers all around them and also far, far away. There was something about that voice that made John look at it with Face Eleven, Can It Be That Bad? "Not only can I hear you, I can smell you," said the voice of Soonchild. "You smell like Sixteen-Face John, my daddy."

When she said that it suddenly hit John that he did not have a Daddy Face. He felt as if he had dropped several feet and landed hard. "Such a big voice!" he said.

"This is a big thing," said the voice of Soonchild.

"What's a big thing?"

"What I'm going to tell you."

John must not have been noticing the whispering in his head for a while, because now it suddenly seemed very loud and urgent, and before he knew it he was at Face Thirteen, I Believe It. "How's everything with you?" he said. "All well?"

"No," said her strange near-and-far voice.

"Aha!" said John. "Oho! What's the matter?"

"I don't know, but something's wrong. How is it where you are?"

"Well, you know," said John, "it's pretty much the same

as always around this time of year. Probably I'll be doing some fishing this week."

"What's fishing?" said Soonchild.

"You don't know about fishing?"

"Not yet."

"The rivers and the sea?"

"No."

"Oh, boy," said John.

"What?" said Soonchild.

"I guess there's a whole world out here you don't know about."

"Tell me about it, Daddy," said Soonchild.

"Well," said John, "there's the sea, and in the sea are the seal and the walrus and the narwhal and the beluga whale and the char and the cod and the other kinds of fish."

"Say more," said Soonchild.

"There's also the land," said John. "This is the time of the melt and the musk-ox and the caribou are on their summer pastures. The hare and the lemming are plentiful, there's good hunting for the wolf, the fox, the owl and the raven. In the snowy places the ice-bear mothers are bringing their children out of their dens and into the sunlight."

"Say more."

John stuck his head outside the hut. "The wind and the earth smell of summer," he said. "The sky is bright. All the birds are nesting: the tern and the gull and the barnacle goose on their cliffs, the raven on its solitary crag, the snowy owl on the stony ground. All these bird-children will be coming out into this world with so many things in it that I can't possibly tell you all of them. But you'll see for yourself when you come out."

There was a long silence except for the whispering in John's head. Then Soonchild said, "I don't think I'm coming out."

John took a deep breath and let it out again, *Hoo.* "Why not?" he said.

"I don't believe there's a world out there."

"This is your father talking. Have I ever lied to you?"

"I don't know."

"Why don't you believe there's a world out there?"

"I don't hear any songs."

John felt as if the bottom had just dropped out of his stomach. The whispering in his head thickened into a heavy buzz and he was seeing colors and shapes that had no names shooting past him. He was seeing great white hollow spaces full of emptiness and blackness, he was seeing endless blackness with no time in it and dry red places with everything dancing and nothing alive. In and out of the whispering and buzzing in his head he thought there might be something else but he didn't know what. "What did you say?" he said to Soonchild.

"I said I don't hear any songs."

21

"No songs?" said John.

"No songs."

"What songs are you listening for?"

"I'm listening for the song of the sea, the song of the seal and the walrus, the narwhal and the beluga whale and the char and the cod and all the other fish. I'm listening for the song of the melt, the song of the musk-ox and the caribou and the summer pastures. I'm listening for the song of the hare and the lemming, the wolf and the fox. I'm listening for the song of the ice-bear mothers and their children. I'm listening for the song of the summer wind, the summer earth and the bright sky. I'm listening for the song of the tern and the gull and the barnacle goose, the owl and the raven on their nests. I'm listening also for the songs of all those other things that are too many for you to tell me about."

When Sixteen-Face John heard this he knew he was looking at the big one, the one that maybe was going to finish him altogether because he had no face that could handle it.

No Problem took one look at him and said, "What's your problem?"

John pointed to her belly and put his finger to his lips. Then he took her aside and said in a confidential tone, "These songs that Soonchild doesn't hear are the World Songs."

"What are World Songs?"

"My father, Go Anywhere, told me about them," said John, "the same as his father, Whatever Works, told him. The world is made up of ideas that live in the Mind of Things but before the idea comes the song. In these songs are such things as the taste of starlight on the tongue, the colors of the running of the wolf, the sound of the raven's blackness, the voices of blue shadows on the snow, the never-stopping stillness of sea-smoothed stones, and the memory of ancient rains that filled the oceans. Without those songs there would be no world."

"I've never heard those songs," said No Problem.

"You've heard them but you don't remember them. These songs are heard only by children in the belly— that's why they come out into the world—the songs are so wonderful and so enticing. Once the children have the actual world in front of them they forget the songs, it would be too sad to remember them—the children would die of sadness because the world has so many bad things in it that aren't in the songs, only soonchildren hear these songs, no one else."

"Then why doesn't Soonchild hear them?" said No Problem.

John didn't answer her.

"Well?" said No Problem. Then she saw that John had gone into a trance. He was standing up but he slowly slid down to a sitting position against the wall. So No Problem left him to it and got busy with her *kamik* work.

WHAT MR. UGLY TOLD JOHN

In his trance John went small, and small he went down to the hole between the rocks where he'd hidden the ugly figure he had carved. Now he was the same size as Mr. Ugly.

"Well, Mr. Ugly," said John.

"Well what?" said Mr. Ugly.

"Tell me straight," said John. "Are you John or are you UnJohn?"

"What do *you* think?" said Mr. Ugly with a whalebone sneer.

"You don't really look like me," said John. "You're as ugly as a whole year of bad luck."

"You carved me."

"I must have been in bad shape when I did it."

"What, you're in good shape now?"

"Don't get smart with me, Ugly. You are definitely UnJohn."

"Prove it," said Ugly.

John didn't know how he could do that. He came out of his trance and found himself sitting on the floor with his jaw aching from clenching his teeth. "Oh, boy," he said.

"What?" said No Problem.

"Can't talk," said John. His mind was jumping from one thing to another. You're the only one there is, Deepguy had told him. And so is Soonchild, thought John. She's the only Soonchild there is and I'm the only father and maybe I'm really UnJohn, and Soonchild doesn't hear the World Songs because I'm jamming them somehow, I'm not letting the World Songs get through to her.

"Aiyee!" said No Problem. They'd been married for a long time and she could read his thoughts. "If she's the only Soonchild there is and she doesn't hear any World Songs maybe the world has gone away because you're UnJohn."

"Don't say that," said John. "Look around you at our hut, at the co-op, at the boats and sleds and skidoos. There's world all around us."

"Maybe it's a *ngoar* world, an imitation world," said No Problem, "*sinnektomanerk,* a dream."

"Stop talking like that," said John. "You're building a bad-luck igloo around us."

"Aiyee!" said No Problem. "If you're really our local shaman and not UnJohn, do something before we wake up nowhere with nothing."

"Quiet, please," said John, "I'm trying to concentrate."

"Sorry," said No Problem. "I'm giving you a hard time

26

when you're already having a hard time. I'll make you some Bye Bye tea so you'll have a good night's sleep and in the morning you'll be ready for whatever you have to do."

"Bye Bye won't cut it," said John. "I'm going to have to do Big Dream."

"Have you ever done Big Dream before?" said No Problem.

"No," said John, "I haven't."

"It could be dangerous," said No Problem. "Be careful."

"I can't be careful," said John. "That's part of it."

"Where will you do it?"

"Out in the open. First I have to pick the right Dream Brew."

"I'll leave you to it then," said No Problem. "Good luck, and whatever happens I'm with you, John."

"I'm already lucky to have you, you're a good wife."

"Thank you," said No Problem, "but let's not get soppy. I'm off to bed and you've got your Big-Dream Business to do." Then she kissed him. John couldn't remember the last time she'd done that.

JOHN'S BIG-DREAM BREW

John went to a walrus-hide box in which were eight seal-skin pouches. He had these from his mother, Stay With It, his father, Go Anywhere, his mother's mother, Never Give Up, his father's mother, Do It Now, his mother's grandmother, Where Is It?, his father's grandmother, Don't Miss Anything, his mother's grandfather, Everything Matters, and his father's grandfather, Go All The Way.

These pouches contained common things like fish eyes, walrus whiskers, powdered narwhal horn, dried caribou afterbirth, ice-bear claws and other things that John didn't even know the names of. By themselves they didn't do anything but when they were combined in various ways they did various things.

Two of the pouches seemed to jump into his hands and those were the ones he decided to go with: the ones from Everything Matters and Go All the Way. Working with a little hand-written manual John mixed the ingredients for a strong brew, said his shaman words over the kettle, and put it on the boil. While he waited he put on his hunting clothes. Then he drank the Big-Dream Brew, went outside, tasted the starlight on his tongue, and said, "Here I am with no faces." The whispering in his head shouted loud and clear, "NO-FACE JOHN!" Then his head went quiet and John lay down and fell asleep.

JOHN'S BIG-DREAM TRIP

The colors were all strange and strong and they hurt John's ears a little and he had to look twice to see what he was looking at. John was walking on the shore because

28

he needed to hear the silence and the sighing of the sea, he needed to see the long deep dark of the sea and the near and far light in the sky. He needed to smell the salt and the oldness and the danger of it. Most of all he needed to think and he was having a hard time doing it.

As he was walking on the old stones of the shore, the gray and sea-worn rocks of it, John had the feeling that someone in the animals of him wanted to talk to him but he couldn't remember what Stay With It and Go Anywhere had taught him about putting himself where the animals of him could reach him. He got himself into several different positions and made passes with his hands. "Hoo!" he said. "Hai!" He twisted himself into something like a knot and said, "Nyuh!" Nothing happened. Two gulls flew by and laughed at him. Their whiteness reminded him of something but he didn't know what it was. He closed his eyes and saw blue-green in his mind.

John kept his mind fixed on the blue-green as he walked on the shore. The sea sighed and the gulls cried but he didn't say anything because he didn't want to miss whatever was coming to him. He came to a place where there were big gray rocks shaped into curves and hollows by the sea. Almost he remembered talking to someone in this place but he couldn't remember who it was.

John kept thinking blue-green and he thought he heard the beating of a drum. It sounded like a drum he knew and he followed the sound of it to the dark place

between the two big rocks above the tide line where he had hidden the John-UnJohn figure. "Funny, how this place seems to follow me around," he said.

He looked into the darkness and saw his old shaman drum that he hadn't used for a long, long time. The seal-skin drumhead was all loose and floppy. He'd left the drum and the stick there when he'd started drinking Coca-Cola and reading magazines with centerfolds.

John tightened the drumhead and took the stick in his hand. The stick began to beat the drum very softly. John felt the vibrations going up his right arm and he heard the drum talking to him. The drum was telling him what to sing so he sang it but not very loud, almost under his breath:

Here I am, nothing else, nobody but me, singing,
"Talk to me, talk to me, talk to me, someone."

The sky wasn't blue anymore, it had gone all gray. This was summer in the North but there was a cold gray wind. "Are you sure about this?" the wind was saying. "Are you sure you want to get into this? Feel me in your belly with the Coca-Cola, Big Fear Man."

John kept singing:

Here I am, all alone, here I am listening.
Here I am singing, "Does anyone have
    anything to tell me?"

John had forgotten what he'd been taught but without knowing it he was singing to the animals of him. He was singing to the hunter and the hunted, he was singing to everything in him that lived deep, deep down and way, way back where the strangeness was. The first voice that answered him was the far-away howling of Pretty Wolf, Arnak Amarok, the she-wolf of No-Face John. It started low and it went up high and shook and trembled and fell away into silence. It had the cold white moon in it and the lost world and the strangeness of life that the spirits don't understand any more than the rest of us. When the lonesome dead heard the howling of Pretty Wolf they all joined in, so there was a whole lot of howling going on.

Then John heard a flapping and a fluttering and Old Man Raven was standing in front of him looking like a hundred years of blackness and a lot of laughs. "Hey,

John," he said. "How's it going?" His voice was as rough and craggy as the stony ledge where he roosted.

"I don't know," said John.

Old Man Raven cocked his head to one side, taking in the howling. "Those dead guys always want something," he said.

John was listening but it was just howling to him. "How can you tell they want something?" he said.

"They're howling, 'John, John, do it, John. Go, John, go,'" said Old Man Raven. "Sounds like they're rooting for somebody called John."

"It does?" said John.

"Now," said Old Man Raven, "they're howling, 'John's gonna do it, John's gonna do it. Yay, John!' They seem to have a lot of confidence in this John."

"Takes all kinds," said John. He didn't want to hear praise, it was unlucky when he hadn't yet got a result.

"I think maybe I'll go somewhere," said Old Man Raven. He turned his head and flashed the little blue mirror that was at the back of his eye. Then he got very big or John got very small and he was in Old Man Raven's left eye looking out. Then he was Old Man Raven himself and he felt his wing muscles working his big black wings as he took off and flew over the white aloneness on the inside of the night.

Being Old Man Raven, John could feel the blackness of his wings going out from him like radio waves, *weeyu, weeyu, weeyu.* He was sending his blackness in

32

all directions and at the same time he was picking up all kinds of signals—jokes and stories, the latest news and weather and more encouragement from the lonesome dead. "Fly it high, fly it low—come on, John, let's go."

Looking from one side to the other of his wings and down at himself what John-Old Man Raven saw was the blue-green skeleton of him working as he flew and glowing like a neon sign, all his light and hollow wing and body bones flapping and steering through the air. He had to laugh at the way his skeleton looked flying on the inside of the night. The dead were flying with him, they kept a steady stream of blackness under his wings that gave him a lot of lift so flying was fun for him. The inside of the night was beautiful, it was full of changing shapes and colors and it sang the story of itself to itself, how strange it all was.

After a while John-Old Man Raven saw Pretty Wolf, Arnak Amarok, down below him trotting on the paths of the living, the paths of the dead with her little black shadow on the white snow trotting beside her in the moonlight. Trotting, trotting, *tsa tsu, tsa tsu, tsa tsu, tsa tsu,* the delicate spirit-bones of her legs were moving sweet and dancingly, the delicate spirit-skeleton of her was fine and thin and blue-green in the whiteness of her and the slanting eyes of her were dark in her sharp face as she trotted on the paths of the living, the paths of the dead.

John could feel how it was with her because he was Pretty Wolf as well as Old Man Raven. He felt the wolf

blood moving in him, he felt his wolf heart beating slow and steady. With his wolf legs he was trotting, trotting, *tsa tsu, tsa tsu, tsa tsu, tsa tsu,* on the paths of the living, the paths of the dead. With his wolf nose he was smelling Old Man Raven. With his wolf ears he was hearing the *weeyu weeyu weeyu* of Old Man Raven's blackness and the howling of the dead and in his wolf mind he was singing a wolf song:

> *Orolooloo, orolooloo, night and night,*
> *Orolooloo, orolooloo, night and night and night.*

Pretty Wolf looked up and saw Old Man Raven. He was bigger now, he was bigger than she was. He started looping the loop and flying upside-down and doing all kinds of fancy flying so she could see that he had lovemaking on his mind.

She told him to come on down and they made love and right away they had a child. Their child was Ukpika, the snowy she-owl, and she was full-grown as soon as she was born.

Then Old Man Raven and Pretty Wolf and Ukpika were gone and John was alone on the gray rocks of the shore with his drum in his left hand and the stick in his right. He was sweating in the cold, gray wind. Now he knew who wanted to talk to him but he was ashamed because he had something to be ashamed of. He beat his drum and he sang:

Ukpika, you with your golden eyes,
You with your face of dreams,
I am not worth talking to
But I am here if you want to talk to me.
Here is John with no more faces,
Here is No-Face John.

John could hear the silence singing in his ears. There was a blue-green glimmering, a blue-green shimmering. The shimmering became golden, became dim, it took on a winged shape, the shape of a woman or a bird that shivered on the air. It was a woman with golden eyes. It was Ukpika, the snowy-owl spirit. John heard her voice, it was low and sad and strange. It was like twilight, like regret, like the lost wind in empty places. "You have not spoken to me this long, long time," she said, "but I remembered you."

"Ukpika the golden-eyed," said John, "what could I say?"

"It's been such a long time," said Ukpika. "Am I really in the same world with Coca-Cola and lotsa hotsa pizza?"

"Yes."

"Is there still a North?"

"You must know there is, Ukpika; there are still snowy owls and all of them are you."

"I'm not sure, sometimes I think I'm only a dream in the Mind of Things." The woman or the bird was fluttering in front of John like a candle flame, sometimes she was only a faint blue-green glow, sometimes she was bright and golden. Her woman face, her owl face was beautiful but if he looked away he couldn't remember it. "Everything is so dim," she said. "Look into my eyes."

John looked into her eyes. The pupils were black and the irises were golden and full of light. He was thinking what a long and wide thing time is, to have so many happenings in it. He was thinking how long the sea and the rocks had been there. He was thinking how hard it was to know what anything is even when it was right in front of you.

"What do you see?" said Ukpika.

"Strangeness."

"Tell me about the strangeness."

"I don't know if I have any words for it. Underneath every thing there is strangeness, there is silence. You are that strangeness and silence in the shape of a bird."

"Yes," said Ukpika. "That is what I am. But does anybody want strangeness and silence anymore?"

John thought about that. Strangeness and silence were what he'd been after when he'd come walking on the shore now but when was the last time he'd wanted them before this? Moons? Years? He was looking down at himself trying to remember how he'd felt when he'd been Sixteen-Face John who knew dreams and trances, magic songs and dances. "I am your local shaman and I know who wants what," he meant to say. But what he said was, "I am your local shamed man and I don't know anything." He was thinking about how it was his fault

39

that Soonchild wasn't hearing the World Songs.

"Did you say 'shamed man'?" said Ukpika.

"I guess I must have," said John.

"Why did you say that?" said Ukpika.

"I am a shamed man," said John, "because of what I did a long time ago."

"You did a thing and from it came another thing," said Ukpika. "That is what life is. Now you are a shaman."

"Shamed man," said John. "I am the only one there is." He was trying to recall what Deepguy had told him.

"The only shamed man?" said Ukpika.

"No. The only one who could handle something big."

"Who told you that?" said Ukpika.

"Mr. Deepguy," said John. "You know him?"

"Yes. Did he tell you what the big something was?"

"No, but the front of it is No Problem's belly and the middle of it is Soonchild not coming out and the back of it is her not hearing the World Songs and I'm her Daddy as well as her local shamed man so it's on me to find them." John sniffled and blew his nose. "Can you help me, Ukpika?"

"Oh, John," said Ukpika, and her voice seemed far away and dim. "It is you who must help me and all the other spirits. Spirits die, you know, and World Songs will vanish if they're not heard by the only Soonchild there is, your daughter."

"Oh, boy," said John, "this is heavier than I thought. Is this still my dream trip and I'll wake up, or what?"

"I don't know," said Ukpika. "I don't think it makes any difference, you just have to face it however it comes to you."

"You're talking to No-Face John," said John. "Have you any idea what I should do and where I should go next?"

"It will come to you, one thing at a time," said Ukpika in a far-away whisper, then she was gone.

WHAT CAME TO NO-FACE JOHN NEXT

"OK," said John. "This is whatever it is and I'll deal with it however I can." As he said that he suddenly had the sensation of being very high up and afraid to look down. There was something like the ghost of a song in his head that he couldn't make out but it scared him. He remembered when he had sixteen faces to handle his scaredness with but those days were all behind him. The very-high-up feeling slowly went away but he still felt it in his stomach.

The feeling in his stomach reminded him that he was hungry. He put his hand in his pocket and found six Baby Ruth bars. His rifle was slung on his shoulder so he knew this was a hunting trip. He was out on the ice looking for seals' breathing holes. For a long time he found nothing, then he saw paw prints and he checked that his rifle was loaded and felt in his ammo pocket for reserve cartridges. Then he looked up and there was Nanuq, the ice bear, very big.

John wasn't getting any blue-green effects.

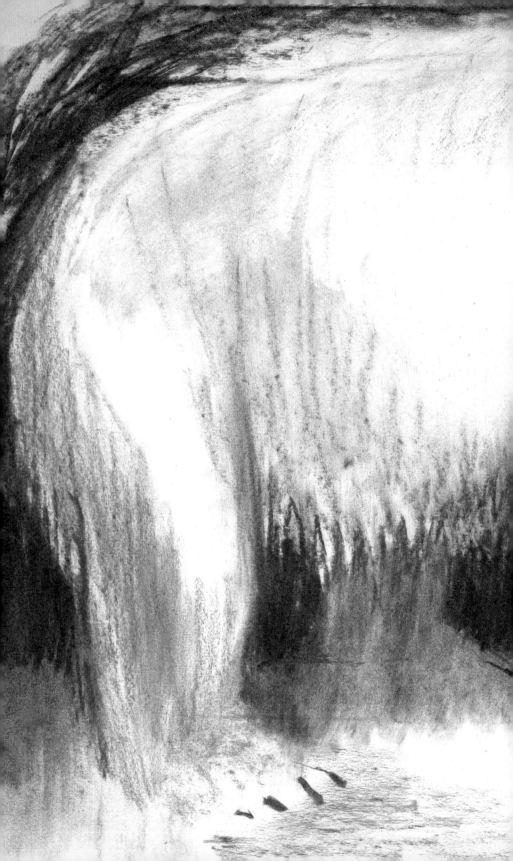

"You're not a spirit then," said John to Nanuq.

"No," said Nanuq. He got up on his hind legs in his I'm-Gonna-Mess-With-You stance. "I'm the real thing, and hungry. Wow, that's one serious smell coming off you."

Funny, thought John. Ukpika didn't seem to notice it.

"So tell me," said Nanuq, "what kind of man are you anyhow?" He wasn't coming closer but John had his finger on the trigger of his Stoppem 275 Magnum. "I'm a shamed man," he said.

"Interesting," said Nanuq. "But the meat is meat and I'm a carnivore."

"So am I," said John. "Plus you'll make a Grade A ice-bear rug for export."

"You're talking big because you're carrying a heavy piece," said Nanuq. "What is it, 275 Magnum or so?"

"You know your guns," said John. "Lady ice bears call this one 'The Widowmaker.'"

"Makes you a big man, does it?"

"Makes me an ice-bear rug exporter."

"Makes you Mr. No-Idjuks," said Nanuq.

"Who you calling No-Idjuks?" said John.

"You," said Nanuq. "You're a big man with your gun in your hand but I think you haven't got what it takes to lay that cannon down and step away from it and go face-to-face with me."

"That's what you think, is it?" said John. He was stalling for time.

44

"That's what I think, because I'm a better man than you are Mr. No-Idjuks."

"Maybe you'd like to put your money where your mouth is," said John.

"Talk plain," said Nanuq.

"You don't seem very quick in the head," said John. "I'm saying what do you bet I won't do it?"

"Anything you want. Name it."

"I'll do that after. Anyhow, this is no big deal. I mean it's part of my Dream Trip, right?"

"You can call it whatever you want, but if I eat you, you're long gone and no waking up. Now are you doing this or are you backing down?"

As far as John could see, if he went face-to-face with Nanuq his name was lunch. On the other hand, Ukpika had made it clear that everything depended on him. *Oh, well,* he thought, *I've had a good life.* Too bad this might be the end of it. He looked up at the smiling blue sky and said, "Tell Soonchild that Daddy stayed with it and went all the way."

"OK, Mr. Big Talk," he said. He laid his Stoppem 275 on the ice and stepped away from it. When he did that he was so scared that his smell went to something like the 275 Magnum version of itself and it hit Nanuq so hard that he almost fell over backward.

"You cheated!" he said with tears in his eyes. "That's chemical warfare!"

45

"Ain't nobody here but us shamed men," said John. He was thinking that Soonchild could be proud of her Daddy now.

"All right," said Nanuq. "Name your claim. I always pay up when I lose."

John didn't know what to ask for, he hadn't thought that far ahead. Time stood still for him. He saw the dim and fluttering flame that was Ukpika. The flame brightened and the beautiful owl-woman came close and whispered something in his ear.

Time started moving and Nanuq said, "Well? Have you gone into a trance?"

"I'm claiming the Blue-Green Password," said John, and it gave him goose pimples to say it.

"Who told you to say that?" said Nanuq.

"It came to me," said John.

"Ukpika told you, and if she's your friend the world needs you. Anyhow we're brothers now."

To be brothers with Nanuq! He, No-Face John the shamed man! *Maybe,* thought John, *I'm not a shamed man anymore.* Nanuq no longer looked as if he wanted to eat him. As big as he was and as dangerous as he was, there was a sadness about him. They stood looking at each other in a new way, then Nanuq said, "Do you have a song?"

"What kind of song?"

"A you song. What's your name?"

"No-Face John."

"So do you have a No-Face John Song?"

"No."

"You can make one up while I sing my Nanuq song," said Nanuq. His voice was different from the voice with which he had challenged John earlier, and his singing voice was different from his speaking voice. Hearing it sent chills up and down John's spine.

THE SONG OF NANUQ

Far and long and white the silence, the wind.
Deep and wide, blue-green the death in me, like
The sea, like time, like the sorrow of the world.
Mine to carry is the sorrow. I can bear it.

Then John sang:

THE SONG OF NO-FACE JOHN

Hungry my answers,
Questions escape me.
Mostly I'm wrong.
This is my song.

"So now we have sung ourselves," said Nanuq.

"Yes," said John.

"Brother, you're not with me," said Nanuq. "Where are you?"

"I was thinking about what you said before we went face-to-face: that if you ate me I'd be dead—it didn't matter if I was sleeping or waking when you did it."

"Well?"

"I get confused. I don't know from one minute to the next whether what's happening is my Dream Trip or reality."

"You're a shaman, John. You should know that a Dream Trip is real. Everything that happens is real and it really doesn't matter what kind of real."

"I used to know all kinds of things but now I don't know anything for sure."

"Listen to me, John, and know this: you've got serious work to do and everything is on you. You're the only one there is, so you can't be half in and half out of where you are. Wherever you are, you've got to be altogether in it. Do you understand?"

"Yes," said John. He felt like a child with Nanuq for a father.

"We're all depending on you, No-Face John."

"You're depending on me!"

"We don't need to talk about that. Now I will give you

the Blue-Green Password. It is never to be written down or spoken aloud. Now I whisper it to you."

John felt Nanuq's breath on his face as Nanuq whispered in his ear. His breath smelled fishy.

When John heard the Blue-Green Password it was as if his mind opened up and went very wide to the right and left and very deep to the front and back, so he could see for miles in all directions and he could smell for miles and he could hear the seals at their breathing holes and the walrus drumming under the ice far away.

And he could feel, yes, he could feel the World Songs. He could feel them humming and thrumming the way you can feel a train coming if you put your hand on a rail. He could feel the songs of the sea, the songs of the seal and the walrus and the narwhal and the beluga whale and the char and the cod and all the other kinds of fish.

He could feel the songs of the land. Back home this was the time of the melt and the musk-ox and the caribou were on their summer pastures. He could feel those songs. He could feel the songs of the hare and the lemming and the hunting songs of the wolf, the fox. The owl and the raven. He could feel the songs of the ice-bear mothers bringing their children out of their snowy dens into the sunlight.

He could feel the songs of the wind and the earth that smelled of summer. He could feel the songs of the bright sky and all the birds nesting: the tern and the gull and the barnacle goose on their cliffs, the raven on its solitary crag, the snowy owl on the stony ground. He could feel the songs of all these bird-children waiting to come out into this world that has so many things in it that he could never name them all.

Yes, John could feel all those songs but he couldn't lay his hands on them and he had no idea how to get them back to Soonchild.

"What do I do now?" he said to Nanuq.

"I don't know," said Nanuq.

"But you're like my big brother now and I need you to tell me that kind of thing."

"Look, John, you're the man. I've told you already that we're all depending on you. I gave you the Blue-Green Password and I have nothing more to give. This whole thing is on you, brother, so hitch up your pants and suck in your gut and get busy."

"Have you been talking to Deepguy?"

"Word gets around, John. When you boil up a Big-Dream Brew, you better be ready to drink to the bottom of the cup."

"OK," said John. "I'm going. I just need a minute to collect myself." He closed his eyes and suddenly he had the sensation again of being very high up and afraid to look down. Was there just a ghost, just the faintest shimmer of a song? He leaned toward it and felt himself dropping the way you do sometimes when you're falling asleep. "No!" he said, and pulled back.

"Still there?" said Nanuq.

"All right already, I'm on my way. There always seems to be some really scary thing up ahead."

"That's life," said Nanuq. "And there's no rest when you're dead. Get used to it."

"All right!" said John. "You are some nagger, Nanuq. Your name should be Na-Nag."

"Don't get smart with me," said Nanuq. "Quit stalling and move out."

So John moved out. With his new amplified hearing he picked up the walrus drumming again and he headed that way.

WHEN JOHN WOKE TIMERTIK

When John got to where the drumming had been, it had stopped. Timertik the walrus, the whole ton of him, was hauled out on the ice for his after-lunch nap. He'd eaten 1,023 clams that he'd dug up from the muddy bottom under the ice. He was snoring and belching and breaking wind and sleeping peacefully and John wasn't sure he should wake him. A ton of walrus is nothing you want to get on the wrong side of.

Timertik, though, was not somebody you could sneak up on. He opened one eye and said, "What?"

51

"Sorry to wake you," said John. "I was trying to be quiet."

"I'm a vewy light thleeper," said Timertik. "You have to be theeth dayths. Thereth alwayth thomebody to thneak up on you. Do you mind if we do mind-talking? My tuskth and my mouthtache give me thith embawwathing lithp."

"I don't mind at all," said John, mind-talking. "It's vewy, I mean very, kind of you to give me your time and I really appreciate it."

"You're not after my hide or anything like that, then?"

"No," said John. "Listen to this." And he whispered the Blue-Green Password into Timertik's clammy ear.

Timertik was so impressed that he forgot to mind-talk. "Ah!" he said. "You'we a vewy impowtant pewthon and my houth is youw houth and you'we my bwother. What can I do fow you, bwo?"

"I don't know," said John. "I thought you might have some idea of what I should do next."

"That's easy," said Timertik. "Get in your kayak and start paddling."

"Where to?" said John.

"Doesn't matter. Just keep paddling and something will turn up. Take your harpoon and your rifle, it's a pretty tough crowd out here. But you're the man and you can handle whatever comes your way. You'll excuse me if I don't see you off, I've still got a lot of clams to digest. Good luck, bro." And he was asleep again.

"Oh, I'm sure something will turn up," said John. "I just hope it's nothing really big and carnivorous and in an ugly mood." He took his harpoon and his rifle, got into his kayak, and paddled away. As he paddled he said to himself, "Who am I kidding? Every next thing that happens is another chance for me to get dead."

As he said that he saw this big black dorsal fin cleaving the water with its V-shaped wake pointing toward him like an arrow. "Right," said John. "Big and carnivorous and always in an ugly mood. Yarluk, the killer whale." He heard the water hissing past the sides of Yarluk as he came on like a big black-and-white torpedo with jaws. No time to do anything with harpoon or rifle, and anyhow, one man in a kayak has no chance against a killer whale. The Blue-Green Password can only be whispered, and when Yarluk was close enough for that John would already be crunched like a Baby Ruth. Not that Yarluk even accepted passwords probably, thought John as he took a deep breath and saw Yarluk coming at him in slow-motion with the water hissing past his sides, singing:

Death, death, O yes
Sweet blue-green death,
Tasty, so good yes.

What a horrible way to die, thought John, already in Yarluk's jaws with the wreckage of the kayak. His terror was so complete that as his lungs filled with salty sea water he could no longer think in words, there were only fast-shuffling pictures in his mind: the gray rocks on the home shore, the sky, No Problem on her hands and knees scraping hides, the unknown face of Soonchild, the fluttering golden flame of Ukpika as the darkness closed over him and the fathoms went past him from blue-green to black and in his bursting ears he heard, yes, the World Song of Death.

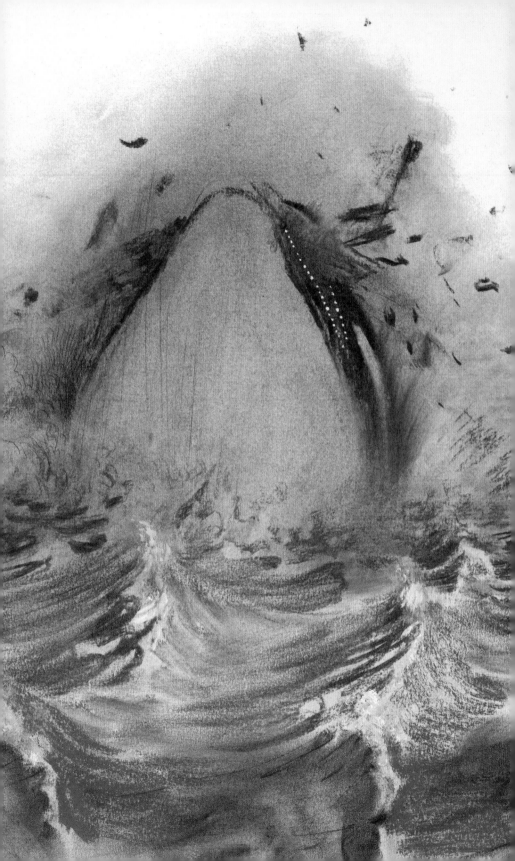

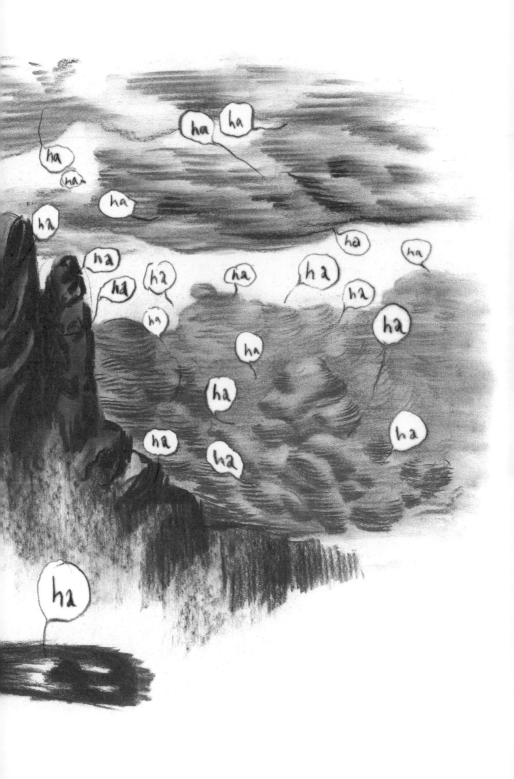

NO-FACE JOHN IN THE LONG WHITE ALONE

When Death let go of him John found himself lying on the ice with his wet clothes freezing on him. "Right," he said, "I died by drowning and this is where I've come to. I thought it would be a busier place, with friends and relatives and maybe something to eat and drink. But this looks like a Long White Alone and I don't like it. It goes on for miles and miles and I have no way to get dry and warm. All I can do is get up and keep walking while frostbite slowly kills me again. Drowning wasn't much fun but at least it was pretty quick. This is scarier than going down in Yarluk's jaws to the deep Death." He looked all around and shouted, "Hello! Is there anybody there?" No

answer, and his voice was swallowed up in the silence and he felt more alone and twice as scared as before.

The Long White Alone was so long and white and alone that it took three moons for a day to pass. It was the worst thing John had come up against and he was pretty sure this would be the end of him. The next thing that happened was that he started remembering. And remembering. And remembering. Very, very slowly. And with pictures in slow-motion.

He was remembering what happened with Ukpika long ago. He was remembering how he became a sha-man. Remembering his anger. Anger at himself and embarrassment. He had shot at a seal and missed and his father, Go Anywhere, had laughed at him. "I don't think you'll be much of a hunter," he had said.

Later, trying to walk off his shame, John had seen a

snowy owl with her little children on their nest on the stony ground. Was she laughing at him? Remembering that from long ago, the golden-eyed she-owl and her children. Were all of them laughing at stupid John? He aimed and did not miss. Long ago he did not miss. Remembering that now in the Long White Alone where it takes three moons for a day to pass.

Remembering those shots that echoed now in his head, the long-ago shots that killed the golden-eyed snowy owl and her children. In the big silence after the shots he heard the sky laughing at him and the rocks and the barnacle geese on their far-off cliffs, all of them laughing at him until the sky and the rocks and the cliffs and the barnacle geese spun around and around faster and faster long ago in John's remembering until everything went black and the blackness swallowed him up. In the blackness the

spirits came one by one to look at him and shake their heads. Looking down at him where he lay as if dead. Then in his remembering the blackness was gone and his father was bending over him.

"Everything went black," said the remembered John.

"What did you see in the black?" said his remembered father.

"The spirits came one by one and looked down at me and shook their heads," said the remembered John and the John in the Long White Alone.

"So now," said his father, father, father echoing slowly, "we have one more shaman, shaman, shaman in the family. Not a good man and probably not a good shaman but good and bad, here he is."

"Here he is," said John in the Long White Alone where not a single day had yet passed since he arrived many

moons ago. He kept walking, there was nothing else for him to do while freezing to death. His face and his hands were black from frostbite and his eyes were frozen shut so that now he walked blind as he died. All the pictures in his head were frozen except the unknown face of his daughter Soonchild. He no longer thought of the World Songs because his thoughts were all frozen.

No-Face John became Dead John and he kept walking because there was nothing else for him to do. He kept walking for years, he never knew how many. Even before his thoughts had frozen he had forgotten all about the World Songs. He had forgotten that he had heard one that was now his. It was the World Song of Death that had come to him when Yarluk the killer whale took him in his jaws down to the black deeps of Death and drowned him.

You have been told that World Songs are what make

the children in the belly want to come out into the world and all the wonderful things in it. What? Is the World Song of Death a song to bring Soonchild out into the world? We must wait and see.

Dead John was walking all blind and frozen but the World Song of Death in him was not frozen. His dead-walking had thawed it out and now it was perking in him like coffee in a coffee pot. The heat of it unfroze Dead John and made the frostbite go away and it brought him back to life so that now he was Live John and more alive than before.

There is a special thing about the World Song of Death: all the other World Songs are in it. Yes, the song of the sea, the song of the seal and the walrus, the narwhal and the beluga whale and the char and the cod and all the other fish. The song of the melt, the song of the musk-ox

and the caribou and the summer pastures, the song of the hare and the lemming, the wolf and the fox. The song of the ice-bear mothers and their children, the song of the summer wind, the summer earth and the bright sky. The song of the tern and the gull, the barnacle goose and the guillemot, the owl and the raven on their nests. Also the songs of all those other things that are too many to name.

How can this be? Why does the World Song of Death contain all the others, and why would that Death Song bring a Soonchild out into the world?

The Death Song brings a Soonchild out into the world to claim all the wonderful things that Death is holding unlawfully, that's why. To defy death and fight for what rightfully belongs to the Soonchildren. That's what brings them out and gives them a proper start in life. The Death

Song is the Master Song and Live John had it in him. He could feel it perking up on him but he didn't know what it was, so he kept walking because he didn't know what else to do.

He was walking, walking, walking when the air around him began shimmering and glimmering, glimmering and shimmering and flickering and there was Ukpika, Ukpika the golden-eyed owl-woman, the golden flame of her fluttering before him. "Go!" she whispered to John. "Go now!"

"Where?" said John.

"To the next thing," said Ukpika.

"What about the World Songs?" said John.

"They are in you now and you must take them to Soonchild before anything stops you."

"The World Songs are in me? All of them? How can this be?"

"Trust me!" urged Ukpika, no longer whispering. "Go!"

THE NEXT THING FOR LIVE JOHN

The dogs were waiting in their gang line, looking back at him with their slanty wolfish eyes. John went to the back of his sled and said, "Let's go." He ran at first to ease the start for the dogs, then he stood on the runners at the back of the sled and shouted "Hup, hup, hup!" The dogs were big strong huskies and very fast. Yes and No were the leaders, Maybe and Maybe Not were swing dogs, This Time and Next Time were team dogs, and This Way and That Way were wheelers.

"Hup, hup, hup!" shouted John. "Yes and No, find trail, let's go!" Yes and No found trail, Maybe and Maybe Not swung the sled into their tracks, This Time and Next Time leaned into their tug lines and pulled hard, and This Way and That Way kept the sled tracking smoothly as they put the miles behind them.

John's nose hairs were stiff with the cold, his eyeballs felt brittle and his breath smoked on the air. "We're heading for home," he said. "And we're carrying the mail, so let's move it, guys." He didn't say what he was really carrying because that would have been unlucky.

As the trees blurred past he had the feeling of being very high up and afraid to look down. He was listening for the ghost of a song that always came with that feeling but what he heard was the howling of wolves. He checked his rifle but he wasn't worried because wolves wouldn't attack him and his team unless they were starving. Besides, no wolf pack was likely to be more than ten wolves and he had eight big tough dogs and a rifle. When his team heard the wolves they leaned into their lines and took off as if the devil were after them.

"What," said John to Yes and No. "Are you expecting trouble?"

"Yes," said Yes.

"Yes," said No.

"But we can outrun them or if it comes to a fight we can handle it, right?"

"Maybe," said Maybe.

"Maybe not," said Maybe Not.

"What's so special about this pack?" said John.

"They're *tonrar amaroks,*" said Yes.

"And Hungry," said No.

"Ghost wolves?" said John. "Ghosts of wolves?"

"No," said Yes.

"No," said No.

"Then what are they?" said John.

"Ghosts of you," said Yes. All the dogs were still going flat out.

"Ghosts of *me!*" said John.

"Ghosts of you," said Yes and No together.

"Why?" said John.

"Who knows?" said This Time.

"Could be anything at all," said Next Time.

"That's not fair," said John, but he had a sneaking suspicion that the ghost wolves were something out of his past. Maybe things as small as the time he hadn't given Joe Little Guy his fair share of the seal meat when they'd hunted together. Or the time he promised Annie Easy a pair of ivory earrings if she'd do what he wanted and he'd only given her a cheap necklace from the co-op. All those little things over the years could add up to quite a few ghost wolves. "But every little thing!" said John. "That's really too much."

"Grow up," said all the dogs. Some of them were laughing at him as they ran. Flat out.

"What is this?" said John. "Are you with me or not?"

"Whatever you say," said the dogs, snickering as they ran.

John looked back behind him and now he saw the wolves. There must have been hundreds of them, trotting *tsa tsu, tsa tsu* on the tracks of Live John. The dogs were going flat out and the wolves were only trotting but they kept up with the dogs with no trouble.

"So the ghost wolves keep coming and we keep running?" said John.

"That's it," said Yes.

"Flat out," said No.

"All right, so we'll get home faster," said John.

"No," said Yes.

"No," said No.

"Why not?" said John.

"Time loop," said Yes.

"Time loop!" said John. "Gimme a break. What's a time loop, for goodness sake?"

"Ask yourself, what does it sound like?" said No.

"Like you keep running and never get anywhere," said John.

"You got it," said Yes.

"But we're carrying the mail," said John.

"How do we break out of this time loop?"

"Don't ask us," said the dogs. "You're the one who's in charge here."

"Maybe he'll think of something," said Maybe.

"Don't hold your breath," said Maybe Not.

"Stop," said John.

"Stop what?" said the dogs.

"Stop running," said John. "I have to go into a trance."

"We can't stop running," said the dogs. "The wolves are right behind us."

"When we stop, they'll stop," said John. "Trust me, they're my wolves and they'll wait until I'm out of my trance."

"What if they don't?" said the dogs.

"You're wasting time," said John. "You yourselves said that I was in charge, so just sit tight and don't talk to strangers while I'm in my trance." And he started getting into it.

"What if this is a dream?" said Maybe to Maybe Not. "Can he do a trance in the middle of a dream?"

"A trance is a trance," said Maybe Not, "wherever it happens."

"Maybe he's just sleeping," said Maybe.

"So let him sleep," said Maybe Not. "And we can take a break until he wakes up."

While the dogs were arguing, John was on his way to visit his great-grandmother, the shaman Where Is It? He figured that women were more outside of time than men were, so his best bet for help with the time loop would be Where Is It? She was his favorite dead relative and a top shaman. When he showed up at her place she was playing poker with some neighborhood spirits. John wasn't sure what they were using for chips, and he didn't like to ask.

"Long time no see," she said to John. "But I know you'll have some kind of good excuse, like you forgot how to do a trance and a dog ate your shaman handbook. Or maybe you've been out of your head for a couple of years."

"Dear Anyanatsiark," said John, "I have no excuses. I am not a good man but I am trying to do a good thing."

"This could take a long time," said Where Is It? to her friends, "so I'll cash in my chips now."

John couldn't make out what she was getting for her chips but he didn't ask. "See you next time," she said to her friends.

"We'll use *my* deck next time," said one if the spirits. John hadn't seen any of them clearly and he didn't recognize their voices so he didn't know who they were.

"OK, tell me about this good thing," said Where Is It? to John. "But maybe you'd like to wet your whistle first. You look like you've been having some hard traveling."

"Have you got any Coca-Cola?" said John.

"Sorry, it's all spirits here. I've got some vodka in the icebox."

"I don't think I can handle the hard stuff. Maybe some tea?"

"You got it," said Where Is It? She put a little spirit-lamp on the table and brewed him some kind of tea that he didn't recognize the smell of but he drank it and felt spiritually refreshed. Where Is It? poured herself a large vodka and lit a small cigar.

"I've been on a really serious trip," said John. "I won't bore you with the details but I got dead twice and I'm not dead sure I'm alive now."

"You always were a wild one, Johnny. Go ahead, bore me with the details."

"Maybe later. Right now the problem is a time loop. I was on my way home with the dogs going flat out and I was carrying the mail . . ."

"Wait a minute," said Where Is It? "You know what you're saying?"

"Yes, I know what I'm saying. And as I said, I was on my way home going flat out because I had to get them to Soonchild so they'd bring her out into the world."

Where Is It? downed her vodka and poured herself another one. She put out the cigar. "What," she said, "she said she wouldn't come out?"

"That's what I'm trying to tell you, Anyanatska. She said she wasn't hearing them. So all right, it was on me to get them because I was the only one there was. And I did it, I got dead twice but I got them and I was on my way back going flat out when we hit this time loop."

"You were running and running and not getting anywhere?"

"That's it. What *is* a time loop anyhow?"

"It's something that comes from unfinished business."

"Say more, please."

"Suppose you're having an argument with a really tough customer, OK?"

"OK, I've had that kind of thing."

"And maybe you say something and this guy says, 'Prove

it' and you can't. So Mr. Ugly has got you stumped, right?"

"Anyanatska, you know everything!"

"I don't miss much. You couldn't find anything to say to Mr. Ugly so all you could do was walk away, *utsa putsa, utsa putsa,* right?"

"That's what I did, I walked away, *utsa putsa.*"

"And that was like the tail of the matter."

"Tail or tale?"

"Tail like what's on the other end of your head. This tail waited for your reply to join up with it. When it didn't, the tail curved over and joined up with itself and made a what?"

"A loop!"

"A loop of that time, John boy."

"A time loop, Anyanatska. Thank you!"

"You're welcome, Johnny Dear. You know what to do now?"

"Do I ever! I'm off now. Can I bring you something on my next visit? A box of cigars maybe?"

"Thanks, but I only smoke El Otro and I get those at the Dark River co-op a little way down the whimmy-whammy. Just bring yourself and don't wait so long next time. Good luck! Vaya con Dios!"

"That's not Eskimo talk, Great-Granny."

"This place is full of foreigners—I can speak forty-seven languages now."

"You're really something, Gran. See you."

HOW JOHN TOOK CARE OF THE TIME LOOP

In his trance John went small, and small he went down to the hole between the rocks where he'd hidden the ugly figure he had carved. Now he was the same size as Mr. Ugly.

"Well, Mr. Ugly," said John.

"Well what?" said Mr. Ugly.

"Tell me straight," said John. "Are you John or are you UnJohn?"

"What do *you* think?" said Mr. Ugly with a whalebone sneer.

"You don't really look like me," said John. "You're as ugly as a whole year of bad luck."

"You carved me."

"I must have been in bad shape when I did it."

"What, you're in good shape now?"

"Don't get smart with me, Ugly. You are definitely UnJohn."

"Prove it," said Ugly.

"You want proof?" said John. "I'll give you proof." He grabbed UnJohn and wrestled him up out of the hole between the rocks. Then he went big and took UnJohn in his hand and laid him on a flat rock. Then he picked up a big rock with both hands and smashed UnJohn to whalebone powder. "How's that for proof?" said John. Then he went back to where his dog team was.

The dogs had just settled down for a snooze when John showed up. "Let's go, guys!" he said. "Everybody up! Hup, hup, hup!"

"What about the time loop?" said the dogs between yawns.

"What time loop?" said John.

"What about the wolves?" said the dogs.

"What wolves?" said John.

The wolves were gone.

"Hup, hup, hup!" shouted John. "Yes and No, find trail, let's go!" Yes and No found trail, Maybe and Maybe Not swung the sled into their tracks, This Time and Next Time leaned into their tug lines and pulled hard, and This Way and That Way kept the sled tracking smoothly. John and his team were putting the miles behind them again and heading for the next thing lickety-split.

WHAT THE NEXT THING WAS

As he stood on the runners at the back of the sled John was thinking *OK, he had the World Songs in him, but how was he going to get them to Soonchild?* Thinking that thought he suddenly became dizzy as the very-high-up-and-afraid-to-look-down feeling hit him. But this time it wasn't just fear, it was sheer sickening terror.

Where were the dogs? What dogs?

There was a rock face in front of John. He tilted his head back and looked up, up, up and he couldn't see an end to it. "No," he said. "Please not. Not this," because he was already up there on a tiny ledge, too terrified to look down. His feet tingled, sensing the drop. His back was against the rock face, he had no room to turn around in and nothing to hold on to. He pressed the flat of his hands to the face of the rock, closed his eyes, and almost lurched forward into empty air before he opened them.

On the ledge with him were four barnacle-goose children, only a couple of days old. They were scared and they were crying. Their parents fluttered near them and told them, "You have to get down to the rocks, then you cross the rocks and the grass to the river where we'll all be safe. We can't carry you down, so you'll have to jump."

"It's such a very long way down," said the children. "And we can't fly."

"You don't weigh much," said the parents. "So you won't hit too hard. You can't stay on that ledge. We've all got to get ready to fly south and every minute counts."

"There are foxes down there," said the children. "And gulls waiting to get us."

"Once you're down we'll be with you while you're crossing the rocks and the grass to the river. Think of the grass—you'll have a good breakfast and then your first swim in the river. Think of the grass and the river."

"We're thinking about the foxes and the gulls and the rocks and the long drop."

"Stop thinking," said the parents. "Jump!"

Before jumping the children sang:

THE JUMP SONG OF THE
BARNACLE-GOOSE CHILDREN

Up here on this high ledge,
Trembling here on the edge,
Now it's our time to go,
Death waiting down below,
Death on the cruel rocks,
Death from the hungry fox,
Death waiting on the stones,
Ravens to pick our bones.
Jump! Into empty air,
Drop to the rocks down there.
Maybe some of us will make it.

Then they jumped.

John didn't dare to look down. He heard the parents down below shouting but he wasn't taking in what they were saying. Pressing his back against the rock face and sick with terror, he felt a terrible urge rising in him. Maybe he was thinking, *if I jump, I'll split open when I hit the rocks and the World Songs will pop out of me and Ukpika or some other friendly spirit will get them to Soonchild. Maybe my Great-Grandmother will take care of it. Maybe my job is done.*

Then, before he could think any more, the terrible urge
jumped

and took John with it.

He was falling,

falling,

falling for

a long time.

This will make three times I've died,
he thought.

As he hit the rocks he thought, *I wonder if the barnacle-goose children made it. I wonder what their names were.* When he split open the World Songs flew out of him. They were all inside the Master Song of Death and they flew out of him like a baseball that's been knocked out of the park. Up and up went the Master Song and it was caught by one of the gulls that was cruising around there.

This gull was not a straight gull, it was an *idluitok,* a bad-person gull. There's a lot of lurking evil in the world and this bird was a bad-lurk bird. Just for laughs, would you believe it, he took the Master Song to Yiwok, the World Swallower. Yiwok is bigger than the world and its job is to swallow the world. Nobody knows what it looks like because it's out-of-sight big. Some say it's all slimy and pulsing like a jellyfish and others say it's a bigger-than-the-world suction that keeps sucking and sucking and sucking.

So anyhow, this *idluitok* gull took the Master Song to Yiwok and popped it like a jelly bean into where he thought the Swallower's intake might be, *Plippo!*

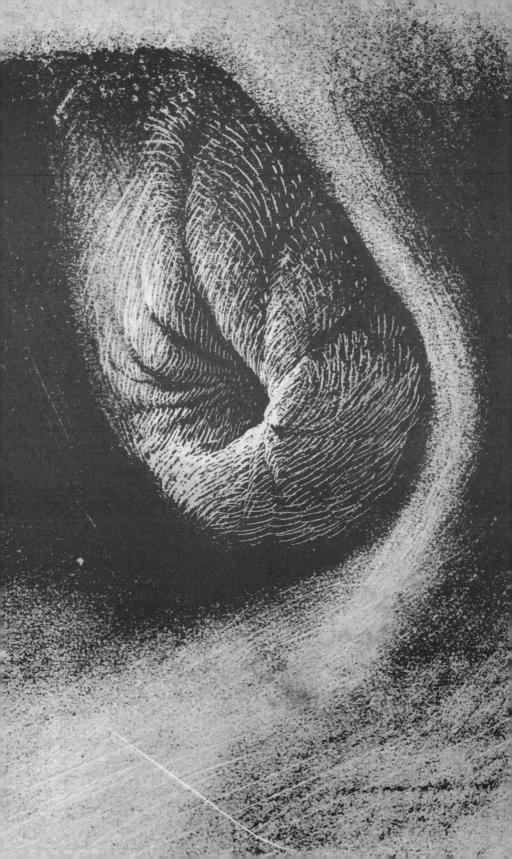

NO REST FOR DEAD-AGAIN JOHN

And where's Three-Times-Dead John? On the rocks at the foot of the cliffs, split open like a gutted fish while the Master Song gets intaken by Yiwok. But as we all know, the dead have no rest.

Remember Deepguy? He likes rocky places and he moves around a lot, so here he is now, looking down at Dead-Again John. "Yo, John," he says. "Wake up!"

No answer.

"John!" says Deepguy. "Rise and shine, let's go!"

"Gimme a break," says John. "Can't you see I'm dead? I'm lying here split wide open."

"So pull yourself together," says Deepguy. "You've got work to do and you're the only one for the job."

"Where have I heard that before?" says John. "What is it this time?"

"It's the World Songs."

"But I already had them in me," says John. "And when I hit the rocks and split open I figured maybe Ukpika or some friendly spirit would grab them and take them to Soonchild."

"You figured wrong, John. When the Master Song flew out of split-open you it was caught by a bad-lurk bird who gave it to Yiwok, the Swallower, so now . . ."

"So now you want me to go and get swallowed and be Four-Times-Dead John! That's really something to look forward to!"

"Be serious, John—it's time to save the world."

"Say that again?"

"It's time to save the world."

"That's heavy talk. You better explain it, I think my brains might be a little scrambled from the fall."

"OK, pay attention now. The world is made up of ideas that live in the Mind of Things, but before the ideas come the songs. In these songs are such things as the taste of starlight on the tongue, the colors of the running of the wolf, the sound of the raven's blackness, the voices of blue shadows on the snow, the never-stopping stillness of sea-smoothed stones, and the memory of ancient rains that filled the oceans. Without those songs there would be no world."

"I know all that," says John.

"Right, and knowing all that, do you want Yiwok to

swallow the Master Song that contains all the World Songs? Is a no-ness of world your idea of a good time?"

"What if it's swallowed the Master Song already?"

"Then you do what you do when you lose something down a hole, you go after it and get it back how you can."

"I don't even know what Yiwok looks like or where to find it."

"You won't find it sitting around here, that's for sure. Sending you in on this job I know I'm leaning on a reed but you're all I've got."

"Right, Coach. I'll do my best."

"Don't let me keep you. I know you want to get started."

"Any idea where I start? Any ideas how?"

"None at all, John. You're the man and you'll have to fly by the seat of your pants. If suddenly there's no more world I'll know you've failed. Good-bye and good luck."

"Thanks a lot for all your no-help," says John. "I'll see you around."

"Sure you will, in this world or some other one."

GETTING READY FOR THE BIG ONE

John figured that he'd get the best advice from Where Is It?, so he did a side trance to pay her another visit. On his way he stopped at the Dark River co-op and bought a box of El Otro cigars and a large bottle of Otherside vodka.

"Thank you, John," she said. "Smoke and spirits, an appropriate gift. And here *you* are. Ready for the Big One?"

"Anyanatska, dear Granny, there was a time when I had sixteen faces and I thought I was ready for anything. Now I'm No-Face Three-Times-Dead John and I haven't been ready for any of the things that have been happening."

"But you stayed with it, and that's what counts. You made me proud, John boy. The whole spirit crowd is here still talking about John's Jump. That was a shot in the arm for all of us."

"John's Jump?" said John.

"When you went off the cliff with the barnacle-goose children; that won't be forgotten while we dead live."

John remembered how he was sick with terror on that very-high-up ledge. He remembered the terrible urge that jumped off the ledge and took him with it. He shook his head, still wondering about it.

"You're trying to explain what made you jump, Johnny, but it can't be explained. It's just what keeps the world going, that's all."

"And Yiwok's trying to swallow it and if it does there won't be any more world."

"And no one to remember us for ever and ever and ever." Where Is It? shivered a little and knocked back about half a pint of vodka. "It's one of those crazy things, like when you read in the paper that the big brains figure the world's going to end in 150 billion years and you think, well, we've got a little time yet. But a week later the big brains change their estimate to 50 billion years and you pull the covers over your head and have a nervous breakdown. Imagine! No more world and nobody to remember there was ever a world. Brrrr! I seem to have emptied this bottle."

"I'll run out and get more," said John. "This could be a three-bottle talk."

"They make them with this bulge inside the bottom so you never really get a full bottle," said Where Is It?

"Be right back with fresh supplies," said John, and was off down the whimmywhammys as fast as he could go.

When he'd come back and his gran had primed herself with a long pull at the second bottle John said, "We were talking about Yiwok. It keeps trying but it hasn't been able to swallow the world yet. Maybe it can't."

"Yiwok hasn't done it yet but it's gaining on us all the time," said Where Is It? "And Yiwok has endless appetite, you can't begin to imagine the endlessness of its appetite. But let's talk about the present. Your job is to get the World Songs back from Yiwok."

"Granny dear," said John, "can you tell me where to start? And I don't really know what Yiwok is or what it looks like."

Where Is It? thought about it for a while. She lit an El Otro and drank some vodka. "This isn't your every-day sort of problem," she said. "It's not like finding a lost ancestor a few centuries back."

"I know it's a tough one," said John, "but you're the best. Other shamans come to you like kids needing help with skinning a seal. If anybody can do it, you can."

"I can't do it all by myself," said Where Is It? "But I'll call a spirit meeting and do a group trance with the girls I play poker with." She hissed something that John didn't catch and the girls appeared, more or less. John couldn't quite see them, and although he heard them well enough he couldn't make out what they were saying. They were

Mostly Never, Erga Werga, and Itsa Bitsa, Who Knows?

"You can watch," said Where Is It? to John. "But don't ask any questions until we come out of it."

"Right," said John, and he stepped back a little to give them room.

The first thing they did was brew up something with a smell ten times worse than John's smell that had rocked Nanuq back on his heels.

After they drank it they sang a song that made John realize that any shaman songs he'd ever sung were kid stuff.

The song was an invitation, he understood that clearly enough because whatever was invited began to turn up in various ways. John couldn't see them with his eyes but he saw them with his mind and he fainted.

John came to with his great-grandmother sitting by him. "We're out of it," she said. "All of us with splitting headaches. Itsa Bitsa threw up and the four of them are sleeping it off."

"I'm sorry it was so hard on you. Did you get anything?"

"You Can't Imagine."

"What can't I imagine?"

"You Can't Imagine is the name of a demon. His full name is You Can't Imagine How Bad and he is no one you'd want to meet in a dark whimmywhammy."

"What's he got to do with Yiwok?"

"Everything. Shall I tell you about it?"

"Yes, please. I need to find out all I can."

"Are you sitting comfortably?"

"I can't remember the last time I was doing anything comfortably."

"I know. It's hard to relax while you're alive. I'll just get a little more of the local spirit down my neck and we're off." After a long *glug-glug-glug* she wiped her mouth and said, "Probably I'll be telling you more than you want to know but you asked for it. The Devil has a shape-up every morning. The demons gather in front of him and he points and says, "You, you, you, and you." He gives work to some and others he passes by till another day.

"You Can't Imagine got the job of swallowing up some people that some other people wanted out of the way. Yes, he was a swallowing kind of demon, and as big as a medium-sized mountain. Off he went, scooped up the people and tried to swallow them but they tasted so bad that he lost his appetite. Are you following this?"

"Yes, Gran, he lost his appetite."

"What I'm saying is that his appetite went off and left him. Bye-bye, he no longer had his yum-yum thingy."

"What happened then?"

"Try to imagine this medium-sized mountain-sized demon appetite yomping off on its own, swallowing everything in its path and getting bigger all the time until . . ."

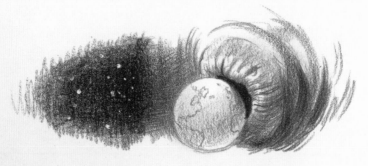

"Until now it's bigger than the world and we call it Yiwok! What does it look like?"

"I suppose it must be something like a bigger-than-the-world mouth: great slobbery lips, an enormous fat tongue, and a throat opening with an uvula in proportion with the rest of it. Just a bigger-than-the-world mouth with nothing at the other end. Swallowing, swallowing everything in the world, makes no difference whether it's dawn over the mountains or a mountain of used cars or young love's first kiss or fifty barrels of beer, in it goes."

"But there's no stomach to receive it, so *where* does it go?"

"I'm not sure I want to know," said Where Is It?

"Anyhow," said John, "the first thing for me to do is find Yiwok. Your name is Where Is It?, Gran. Can you tell me where it is?"

"No, I can't," said Where Is It? "You're the man and this whole thing is on you. The way this job works is that I have to stay out of it, the losing and the finding have to come from you—that's how you'll develop the power you need to get through it."

"Right," said John. Having to take charge of the whole thing himself already made him feel a little more powerful. "Excuse me," he said, "I need to do a speed trance."

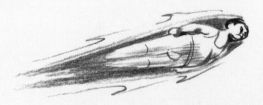

He got into it fast, and as soon as he was in he said, "This is No-Face Three-Times-Dead John calling Old Man Raven. Are you there?"

"Yo, John," said Old Man Raven. "What's up?"

"Big trouble. You want to help me save the world?"

Old Man Raven blinked his little blue eye-mirror. "Did you say save the world?"

"That's what I said."

"Can it be done? I mean, hasn't Yiwok got it pretty well swallowed?"

"Yes, but there's still some left and it's on us to turn this whole thing around."

"Why us?"

"There's nobody else."

"Wow. That's how it is, is it?"

"That's about the size of it. I thought of you because I have a feeling there's a lot of black in this business."

"Messing with Yiwok we could get dead real fast. We could get disappeared like we never happened."

"Am I talking to Old Man Raven or Old Man Chicken?"

"I'm who I always was and I'm the father of Ukpika, so how about a little respect?"

"You got it, old friend, especially if you're willing to have a go at saving the world. So tell me, are you in or are you out?"

"Oh. I'm in all right. Nobody lives forever, and if you get dead trying to save the world it's a nice way to be remembered, except there won't be anybody to remember it. Where do we start?"

"I'm guessing there's like a zone of swallowing somewhere out there and if we head for Black we'll find it or it'll find us, whichever is worse."

Old Man Raven wasn't too eager to head for Black. "I've got nothing against black in itself," he said. "Goodness knows. My middle name is Black, you might say. But I don't feel too easy about heading for Black to find a swallowing zone."

"Get used to it, Rave—can I call you Rave?"

"Whatever flaps your wings."

"So, as I was saying, get used to it. There won't be much easy on this trip. Any idea where to start looking for this swallowing thing?" He didn't like saying the name of it.

"This isn't like finding your freshest neighborhood roadkill, John. I'm going to have to get some help."

"Whatever gives you altitude," said John.

"OK, stand back now—I'm going to disappear into the generations of ravens all the way back to the Original Egg. Be careful not to get sucked into my slipstream." *WEEYOOSH!* And he was gone.

John settled back into his speed trance and waited.

He'd always been scared, he couldn't remember a time when he hadn't been, but all his past scaredness was nothing to what he felt now. Didn't so much *feel* it as just be *in* it. He had come out on the other side of terror into pure desolation. Casting about for something to hold on to he found the little barnacle-goose children on the ledge, scared and crying. "But they jumped," he said to himself. "And you jumped too, No-Face John. Hang on to that."

WEEYOOSH! Raven was back, and his feathers had turned white. "Rave, are you all right?" said John.

"Do I *look* all right? *You* try going back to the Original Egg and see how pretty you look when *you* come out. Just give me a minute to catch my breath." John gave him a minute.

"OK," said Raven. "I went all the way back, and all I have to show for spinning through millions of black raven years is this: we have to look for a suction point."

"Where would that be?"

"If we head in the general direction of Black we'll find it or it'll find us, whichever is worse."

"Like I said. So OK, let's head for Black."

"John?"

"What?"

"I feel like I'm saying good-bye to everything, including myself."

"But that's what life is, Rave. It's one good-bye after another until you reach the Big Hello at the end when That's All She Wrote."

"Why is it all so easy for you, John?"

"It's easy for me because I'm on the other side of terror and into pure desolation. Can we go now?"

"OK, John, look into my left eye."

John looked into Raven's left eye, Raven blinked his little blue eye-mirror and John was in the eye looking out.

"Ready for take-off?" said Raven.

"Ready," said John.

"Any last words or wishes?" said Raven.

"Yeah. Stop talking and start flying."

"Roger," said Raven. He taxied down the runway, raised his wings, gave a big downstroke, and they left the ground behind and were heading for the Black.

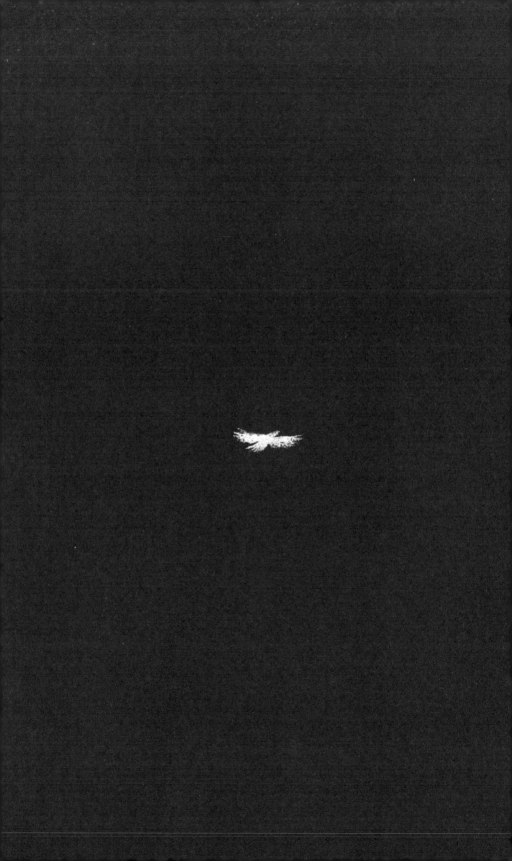

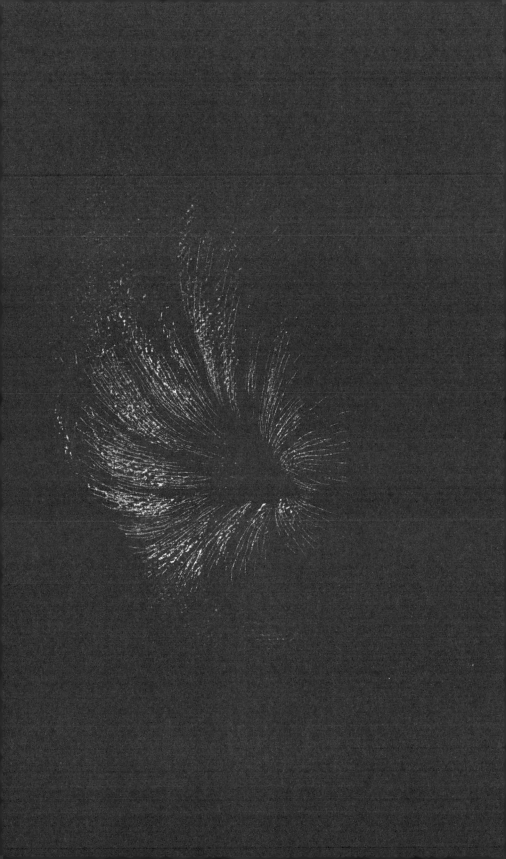

JOHN AND RAVEN GET SUCKED IN

John and Raven didn't have to find the Point of Suction, it came looking for them and it sucked them in. Oh, the wetness of it and the smell! Like some bigger-than-the-world problem with drains, whether blocked or unblocked it would be hard to say. "Wait a minute!" shouted John amid the horrendous ulping and gulping.

"For what?" said Raven. "A belch?"

"We're already being swallowed by Yiwok! I felt us go over a great slobbery lower lip!"

"Duck!" said Raven as a herd of cows scrabbled over them, followed by a tractor, a chicken house, forty or fifty rolls of barbed wire, a symphony orchestra playing a symphony, and two lovers in the act of love.

"We're on the enormous tongue," said John. "Here comes throat and we're going throooouuugh!"

"You don't have to keep telling me what's happening," said Raven as they splashed into what? A sewer? A swamp? Whatever it was, the Master Song with all the World Songs was like a hundred fathoms down and they were going to have to dive for it through muck and murk with very poor visibility.

Each in his own speed trance, John and Raven took turns diving, but after twenty or thirty thousand years they hadn't found anything but rubbish.

"I wonder," said Raven, "if we're going to live long enough to save the world."

"There may be a shortcut," said John.

"Like what?" said Raven.

"I know a song," said John, "that if we sing it, the Master Song might hear it and answer us."

"You really think so?" said Raven. "Let's hear it."

John sang:

THE JUMP SONG OF THE
BARNACLE-GOOSE CHILDREN

Up here on this high ledge,
Trembling here on the edge,
Now it's our time to go,
Death waiting down below,
Death on the cruel rocks,
Death from the hungry fox,
Death waiting on the stones,
Ravens to pick our bones.
Jump! Into empty air,
Drop to the rocks down there.
Maybe some of us will make it.

"It's certainly worth a try," said Raven. "But how can we get it all the way down there to the Master Song?"

"There are lots of rainspouts and pipes of various kinds down there. We'll put them together to make one long tube and we'll sing down it," said John.

That work went fast. In two or three thousand years they had the tube put together and John sang down it. "Listen for an answer," he said when he finished.

They both listened.

"Anything?" said John to Raven.

"I keep getting the symphony orchestra," said Raven. "The brass section."

"All right then, we'll just have to keep doing it until we get through the interference. Eventually the Master Song will answer."

"How can you be so sure?"

"Sooner or later the right question always gets an answer," said John. "And this song is the right question."

So they sang, these two in their speed trances. Through the centuries John became a little old man with white hair and Raven became a little old Raven whose white feathers were starting to fall out. They sang themselves hoarse, they sang until John lost his voice and Raven could only croak.

After fifteen or sixteen thousand years, John said to Raven, "Listen, I think I hear something."

They both listened and they both heard something.

They listened as hard as they could down the tube and they heard it rising toward them *Eeyup! Upty up up!* Slowly through the muck. Ten thousand years more and there it was, yes! The Master Song that contains the World Songs was in John's hand and he quickly popped it into his mouth and swallowed it.

"Now how do we get out of here?" said John to Raven.

"If we can find something for me to stand on I'll do a vertical takeoff," said Raven.

In no time at all they made a raft with a garage door and a couple of oil drums. When the raft was finished, Little Old Raven blinked Little Old John back into his left eye and said, "Ready for takeoff?"

"Ready!" said Little Old John.

No longer little and old, Raven jumped high into the air, raised his wings, gave a strong downstroke, and they left Yiwok behind and were on the way home.

HOW SOONCHILD GOT THE WORLD SONGS

"I'll drop you off now and head for my place," said Old Man Raven.

"Thanks," said John as he set foot on the ground.

"If you need to save the world again, count me in," said Old Man Raven.

"You got it, old buddy," said John.

Old Man Raven took off, buzzed John once, did a victory roll, and was gone.

No Problem was having coffee when she picked up John's landing vibe. She went out and found him curled up among the big rocks on the shore. "Yo, John!" she said. "Drop your trance and take your chance! Smell the coffee, breakfast is ready."

John woke up and smelled the coffee and followed No Problem into the kitchen. The place looked smaller than he remembered. "How'd it go?" she said.

"It went OK."

"Have you got the World Songs?

"Yup."

"How will you make Soonchild have them?"

"I don't know."

"You don't know?"

"That's right, I don't know."

"Oh, boy. You're some shaman, you are."

"I sure am," said John, and he began to laugh.

"What are you laughing at?" said No Problem.

"Don't know," said John. And looking at him, No Problem began to laugh too. She was a big, strong woman with a face that made you not want to make her angry but when she laughed she could light up the darkest place. Looking at her John was seeing the only one of her. He was seeing all that she was. He felt his heart jump inside him and he grabbed his wife and gave her such a kiss that the coffee in the pot started perking again and the Master Song went out of John and into No Problem. The Master Song, the Death Song with all the World Songs in it zipped into No Problem, *voop*!

"Wow!" she said. "Something just went straight to my belly with a *voop*!"

"Well, I *am* your local shaman," said John.

In No Problem's belly Soonchild said, "Aha! Oho! Hey! Gimme that, it's mine!"

"What's happening?" said No Problem.

"I think we'll see in a minute," said John.

Soonchild was fighting the Death Song for the World Songs. She was fighting for what was rightfully hers and she wasn't taking any nonsense from Death.

No Problem and John heard the fighting stop, there was silence for a moment. Soonchild had the World Songs and right away she forgot them and wanted to get out into the world. "Yo!" she said. "Here I come!"

"Aiyee!" said No Problem. "My waters have broken!" But there was no labor, Soonchild popped out with a *zoopity doo* and there she was, a good-looking baby, complete with all her fingers and toes and everything else. John cut and tied the umbilical cord, then he held her up by the ankles and smacked her bottom. Soonchild let out a howl, John turned her right-side up and put her in No Problem's arms and now Soonchild was out in the world like a regular baby. No Problem put her to the breast and Soonchild drank the milk of human kindness and decided to give the world a try.

"Here she is at last!" said No Problem. "I can hardly believe I've finally got my hands on my Soonchild."

"She's not a soonchild now," said John. "She's a here-and-nowchild."

"Maybe that's her name," said No Problem. "Here and Now. What do you think?"

"I think you got it right," said John. "It's been a long haul but she's Here and Now. She's kind of ugly but I guess we'll get used to her." Here and Now was beautiful but John didn't want to say so for fear of calling down bad luck.

"Yes," said No Problem. "We'll just have to get used to this ugly kid." And she and John looked at each other and laughed.

"Just a minute ago she was talking loud and clear," said John, "but now she hasn't got a word to say."

"That's how it is with babies," said No Problem. "It takes a while."

"I wonder what her first word will be," said John. "And I wonder what she'll be when she grows up."

"Do you think she'll be a shaman?" said No Problem.

"Who knows?" said John. "She's the only one of her and she's a mystery."

HERE AND NOW

Here and Now's first word was a whisper.

"Aiyee!" said No Problem. "She just whispered her first word and I didn't understand a word of it."

"Aha!" said John. He came over to Here and Now and he said, "Whisper that again, please."

Here and Now whispered it again.

"Oho!" said John.

"What is it?" said No Problem.

"I think she's going to be a shaman," said John.

"Why do you think that?"

"She just whispered the Blue-Green Password. I had to do a Big-Dream Trip and go face-to-face with Nanuq to get it."

"So how'd *she* get it?"

"It's a mystery to me, and so is she."

"What *is* the Blue-Green Password anyhow?"

"It gets you into places you couldn't get into without it." He was remembering Yarluk's jaws and the Long White Alone.

"Sounds like a shaman kind of thing," said No Problem. "When she's talking properly I'll ask her how she got it."

But when Here and Now was talking properly she couldn't remember how she got it. She liked hanging out with John and she always wanted him to tell her stories. He told her stories about his Big-Dream Trip and he made up some more out of his head. Here and Now loved hearing about Ukpika and Nanuq and Timertik and Yarluk and the Long White Alone and the barnacle-goose children. She made John tell her those stories again and again until they became stories of her own and memories of her own.

From a beautiful baby Here and Now grew into a beautiful girl. She liked to be alone and she liked to walk among the big stones along the shore and make up songs that she tried out on her parents. They were strange songs that she heard in the rocks and the shore, the wind and the sea, and No Problem and John liked them.

Here and Now did not become a shaman. She went to school in the South and she called herself Ukpika. She became a singer and songwriter and she formed a band, The Barnacle-Goose Children, with four college friends, Jake Wilson, acoustic guitar, Zoltan Kertecz, zither, Marigold Atkey, vibes, Jean-Louis Martel, flute, and herself on vocals.

With their first album, *Paths of the Living, Paths of*

the Dead, The Barnacle-Goose Children jumped into the charts at No. 1. *Rolling Stone* said their music "shimmered like the Northern Lights" and *NME* hailed Ukpika as "the new and haunting voice of the North." Their next albums, *Blue-Green Password* and *Long White Alone,* followed the first into the charts and for seven weeks they were 1, 2, and 3. All kinds of people young and old—everyone, it seemed—had ears for The Barnacle-Goose Children, sometimes referred to by DJs as "those hot goslings." Very soon all three albums were available at Ukpika's hometown co-op, along with mugs, T-shirts, little model barnacle geese and larger high-relief ones in flight for hanging on the wall in sets of three.

Ukpika and her band were featured frequently in business magazines as well as the popular press, and *National Geographic* did a photo essay of the forty or fifty huts by the bay. For this the locals organized a whale hunt, some blanket tossing, singing matches, and *umiark* races. So it was a good job all around and *National Geographic* ran a Rolex ad with Ukpika wearing a Rolex Oyster.

Finally, *The New York Times* pronounced Ukpika and The Barnacle-Goose Children "a unique cultural phenomenon unparalleled in popular music."

Ukpika did good things with her money. She built a hospital and a music school for the place by the bay and opened an art gallery in the South for the work of hometown sculptors.

She never married, she said there was no room for that in her life, but despite her many artistic and commercial commitments, Ukpika kept in close touch with her parents with letters and visits. The three of them enjoyed one another's company, always found a lot to talk about, and could pretty well read one another's thoughts.

Every year Ukpika brought the band home with her and did a special concert with No Problem and No-Face John in a place of honor on the stage. She did it every year on the date when Sixteen-Face John had left on his Big-Dream Trip to get the World Songs for Soonchild.